Jesse loved to swim in the water with his best friend Willy. They played hide-and-seek among the rocks and splashed together along the surface. Their relationship was special, because Willy was no ordinary playmate — he was a killer whale.

Jesse turned to Willy as he floated on his back. "I'm so glad Annie and Glen decided to move near the ocean, Willy. Glen loves working on boats and Annie is so busy at the newspaper. It leaves plenty of time for us to have fun!" he said.

Willy splashed his tail on the surface and squeaked with delight, as though he understood everything that Jesse had said.

"I hope you don't mind helping me out at my new job. I think you'll like it. Come on!" Jesse shouted.

Jesse and Willy approached the Misty Island Oceanographic Institute, a research center nearby. They arrived just as Marlene, one of the marine specialists, was beginning to feed the animals in the Healing Pond.

TALKING TO ANIMALS

BASED ON EPISODES FROM ABC'S NEW ANIMATED SERIES

ADAPTED BY NANCY E. LEVIN
ILLUSTRATED BY SEAN GLOVER

SCHOLASTIC INC.

New York   Toronto   London   Auckland   Sydney

To Michael and Joshua

ISBN 0-590-25352-2

Book designed by N.L. Kipnis

12 11 10 9 8 7 6 5 4 3 2 1   5 6 7 8 9/9 0/0

Printed in the U.S.A.   24

First Scholastic printing, March 1995

"The old injured sea lion trick, huh? Sorry, Lucille, only sick animals get fed. Mr. Naugle's orders," Marlene said. Lucille was a sea lion that lived at the institute. She was very curious and always getting into mischief.

5

"This lagoon is called the Healing Pond," explained Mr. Naugle as he led a tour through the institute. Mr. Naugle was the director of the institute. "It's filled with little animals that are injured or sick and need our help. When they are better, they simply swim out to sea."

At that moment, Willy, with Jesse on his back, jumped out of the water and landed on shore right in front of the crowd. Willy roared and everyone screamed in surprise. Mr. Naugle glared at Jesse and Willy. "It's all right. Everything is under control" he assured the people as he ushered them back into the building.

"What's everybody afraid of?" Jesse asked Marlene. "It's only Willy!"

"Willy?" Marlene replied.

"Yeah, he's my best bud," Jesse answered.

"Well, I don't mean to be rude, but you'll have to get your best 'bud' away from the Healing Pond. Animals come here to get help, not to be a killer whale's lunch!" snapped Marlene.

"Aw, Willy wouldn't hurt a fly," Jesse argued. "He's just a big pussy cat, aren't you, Willy?"

Willy "smiled," showing his big razor sharp teeth.

Just then, Randolph, the manager of the institute, walked over. "Ah, Marlene. I see you've met Jesse. He's going to help us take care of the animals here."

"We need all the help we can get, that's for sure. But keep that killer whale away from my babies," Marlene said, pointing to the sick animals.

"Everything will be okay, right, Jesse?" Randolph asked.

"Yeah, sure," Jesse replied, rolling his eyes.

Marlene and Randolph headed over to a truck to unload new supplies and let Jesse finish feeding the animals in the Healing Pond.

Jesse grabbed some fish and turned to feed the animals. Behind Jesse's back, Willy ate the rest. Lucille sniffed at the empty tub and barked angrily. Then she dove into the water and swam toward the open sea.

"Uh-oh. You ate all the fish, Willy!" Jesse exclaimed. "At least there's another barrel over here." Jesse opened the barrel and began to feed some of the other animals. This time, Willy grabbed the entire barrel with his teeth and emptied it into his mouth.

Meanwhile, beneath the Healing Pond, a submarine glided through the water. It was driven by the Machine, a man with a metal cyborg arm and metal skull plates covering half his head. The Machine said, "This is where we are going to dig: the Misty Island Oceanographic Institute, three hundred square miles of government-protected seabed. Untouched since time began."

The machine flexed his robotic arm. "And if that rotten whale shows up, I'll make him pay for what he did to my arm. My whale-seeking torpedo will take care of that bucket of blubber!"He continued, "My cyberbot mining machine can process two tons of gold ore every minute. It'll be like ripping money right out of the earth."

The mining robot began to dig with its huge iron claws. Fish scattered and a cloud of dust rose from the ocean floor. When the dust settled, hundreds of dead fish were floating through the water.

Out in the ocean, Lucille swam along, looking for food. She saw several fish and raced to catch them. The hungry sea lion was about to grab one, when she suddenly found herself face-to-face with a huge machine. It was the mining cyberbot. Spotlights blinded her and in seconds the cyberbot's iron claws grabbed her along with mounds of dirt and loads of other sea animals.

Back at the Healing Pond, Jesse and Willy were horsing around.

"Jesse, we try to keep the Healing Pond . . . safe and peaceful, okay?" Marlene said.

Jesse glanced at Willy. "Sorry, bud, no more cannonball splashes."

Jesse climbed out of the water and sat next to Marlene. "You oughta chill out, Marlene — you know, have a little fun? Do a few cannonballs?" Willy squealed to show his agreement.

"There's no time. I'm working here because I want to make a difference. We need to clean up the ocean before it's too late." She continued, "Every day people dump junk in it: oil, chemicals, garbage. If we keep polluting, soon it will even harm Willy."

"Wow, now I call that serious!" Jesse agreed.

14

When Mr. Naugle came outside, he discovered an empty fish barrel with Willy's teeth marks.

"He's eaten the entire day's supply of fish!" he shouted.

"My Willy?" Jesse replied innocently.

"I know a killer whale's teeth marks when I see them!" Mr. Naugle exclaimed. "We cannot afford to feed a whale here, Jesse. The whale goes, understand?"

Jesse shouted, "If Willy goes, I go!"

"Fine, I'll take you *both* off the payroll," stated Mr. Naugle. Jesse climbed on Willy's back. As they headed out to sea, Willy slapped his tail on the ocean's surface and splashed a big wave all over Mr. Naugle.

"From now on, it's just you and me, Willy. And that's the way we like it," Jesse said. They dove under the water and swam side-by-side along the bottom.

All of a sudden, Willy veered off as if he had heard someone call for help. Jesse followed him and they both saw Lucille lying hurt on the ocean floor. Quickly, Willy scooped the sea lion onto his nose and brought her to the surface. As they broke through, Lucille took a breath, but she was badly hurt.

Jesse took Lucille and calmly reassured her. "It's going to be okay, Lucille, easy girl, eeeeeasy."

Jesse turned to Willy. To his surprise, he thought he heard Willy speak.

"Take her to Randolph, take her to Marlene!"

Jesse's jaw dropped. He did a doubletake at Willy. "Willy, did you just — speak to me?" he cried.

Willy, who was just as surprised, replied, "I always speak to you, but for the first time — we understand each other."

Jesse started to answer when he heard Lucille whine, "Help me . . . machine hurt me . . . please, help me!"

Jesse just stared at Lucille. So Willy scooped both of them onto his back and swam toward the institute.

As he rode on Willy's back, Jesse tried to talk to Willy again.

"Am I losing it, or did you two just . . . talk to me?" he asked. Willy's excited squeaks were the only answer.

"Lucille? Willy? Come on you guys!" Jesse cried. But Lucille and Willy didn't answer. "Oh, well. Must have bumped my head or something," sighed Jesse.

19

At the institute, Randolph and Marlene worked quickly to bandage Lucille's wounds. "Sharks didn't do it. Wonder what she got into?" Randolph asked.

"The important thing is, Lucille's going to be okay," said Marlene.

"Thanks to Jesse and Willy!" Randolph added.

"Randolph, something happened out there. Willy talked to me. Lucille did, too! She said, 'Help me' and something about a machine."

Randolph looked at Jesse. "You heard them? You understood them?" Jesse nod-

20

ded. "It was amazing. But then all the way back, I tried to get Willy to talk again, but all I got were whale squeaks." He hesitated. "So what do you think?"

"You must be one of the 'Truth Talkers,' special kids who can talk with animals. My ancestors have always believed that certain kids have this gift," said Randolph.

"Will I be able to get him to talk again?" asked Jesse.

"To get in touch with your power, Jesse, you must be calm. Breathe slowly. Focus your energy," Randolph advised.

21

"I've been thinking," Jesse announced to Marlene and Randolph. "I want to help you guys. I'm going to ask Mr. Naugle for my job back."

Marlene put her arm on Jesse's shoulder, "come on, rookie, I'd like to show you how we get around in the ocean."

Marlene opened the hatch of the mini-sub and Jesse followed her inside. Marlene fired up the engines and went deeper into the water.

From the window of the mini-sub, something horrible caught their attention. The cyberbot was coming straight at them with its iron claws open!

The cyberbot attacked. "Jam their communications! We can't let them report us!" shouted the Machine, who was controlling the cyberbot from his submarine.

"Randolph! Come in, Randolph!" Marlene screamed over the radio. "It's dead, Jesse!"

"And so are we! What is that thing? Doesn't it see us?" Jesse asked.

"Maybe the flashes will get their attention," Marlene said as she flipped the switch on the outside lights. The lights blinded the Machine and the cyberbot lost its grip.

The damaged mini-sub sputtered away. But the cyberbot caught up to it and clamped onto it again.

"Everyone will think there was a tragic 'accident,' huh?!" chuckled the Machine. Just then, BANG . . . Willy slammed into the side of the cyberbot. The cyberbot keeled over and let go of the mini-sub.

"It's Willy!" said Jesse, looking out of the viewport. But then, they felt the mini-sub sinking. "I can't work the controls!" Marlene shouted as the mini-sub fell toward a deep abyss. It stopped just on the edge. Quickly, the two of them dressed in their scuba gear as Willy banged on the cyberbot.

Willy kept banging his tail on the back of the cyberbot — CRASH! It collapsed into a heap of metal.

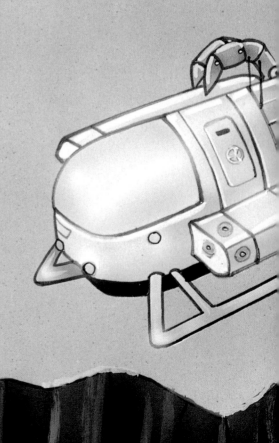

But the Machine was not finished. From the pilot's seat of his high-tech submarine, the Machine gave new orders: "Launch the whale-seeking torpedo immediately!"

Willy saw the missile zooming toward him and he raced off. He dodged around a piece of coral and then made a spectacular leap over a sandbar. KA-BOOM . . . the torpedo exploded into the sandbar.

The Machine quickly steered his submarine away, vanishing into the ocean depths.

Jesse and Marlene were trapped in the mini-sub. "If we fall into the abyss, even these scuba tanks won't save us!" Marlene admitted.

Willy appeared at the window.

"If only I could talk to him!" Jesse thought out loud. Marlene turned on the external speakers. "If you *can* talk to Willy, do it now, rookie!" she yelled.

"What was it Randolph said? . . . Calm down, breathe, and focus." As he concentrated, he said, "Willy, get under us and lift us to the surface."

Willy disappeared from the window. Jesse and Marlene waited and waited . . .

"It's no use!" Marlene confessed.

Then, all of a sudden, Jesse and Marlene felt the sub starting to rise.

"He understood me! I told you he could do it!" Jesse exclaimed.

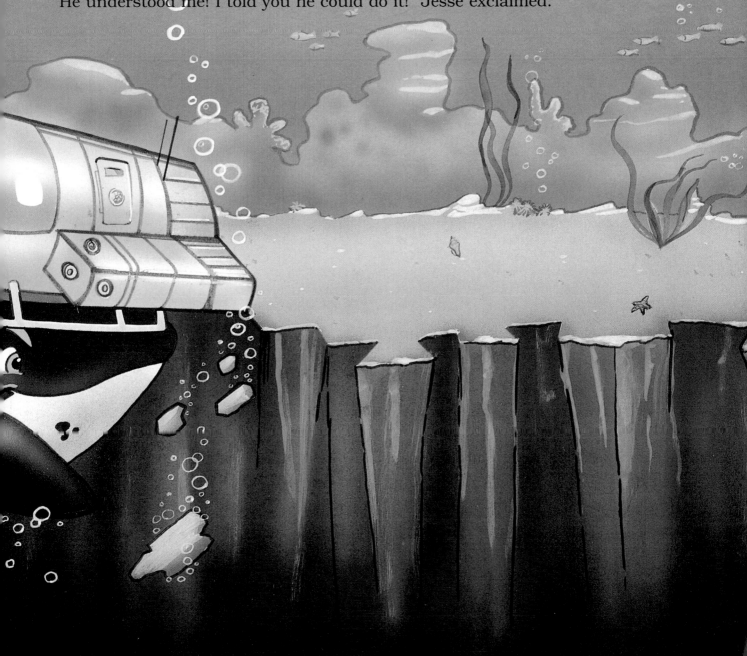

Back at the institute, Jesse, Marlene, and Randolph watched TV as the screen showed pictures of the cyberbot.

"These pictures were taken by the institute's mini-sub. However, no trace of the illegal mining equipment was found," the TV announcer was saying.

"Could have been a terrible accident," Randolph concluded.

"It was no accident. Those guys were after us," Jesse insisted.

"We'd still be down there if it hadn't been for you and Willy! Guess you really *can* talk to him!" Marlene admitted.

"I'm still working on getting *him* to talk to *me*!" Jesse said with determination.

Later that day, Jesse and Willy were floating in the Healing Pond. Jesse tried to stay calm, breathe, and focus in order to talk to Willy.

"Jesse, I understand you," Willy said.

"Finally! I was going loony trying to stay calm," Jesse replied.

"Jesse, I have something important to tell you. The creature that attacked you is called the Machine. My friends and I have been fighting him for years. But now that we can talk to you, maybe together we can stop him!" Willy said.

"Willy, it's dangerous. I mean, we'd be in trouble every minute." Jesse hesitated and then said, "Oh, well. We're always in trouble anyway!"

32